THE MICROWAVE LIBRARY

COOKING WITH

Vegetables

ELIZABETH CORNISH

THE MICROWAVE LIBRARY

COOKING WITH

Vegetables

ELIZABETH CORNISH

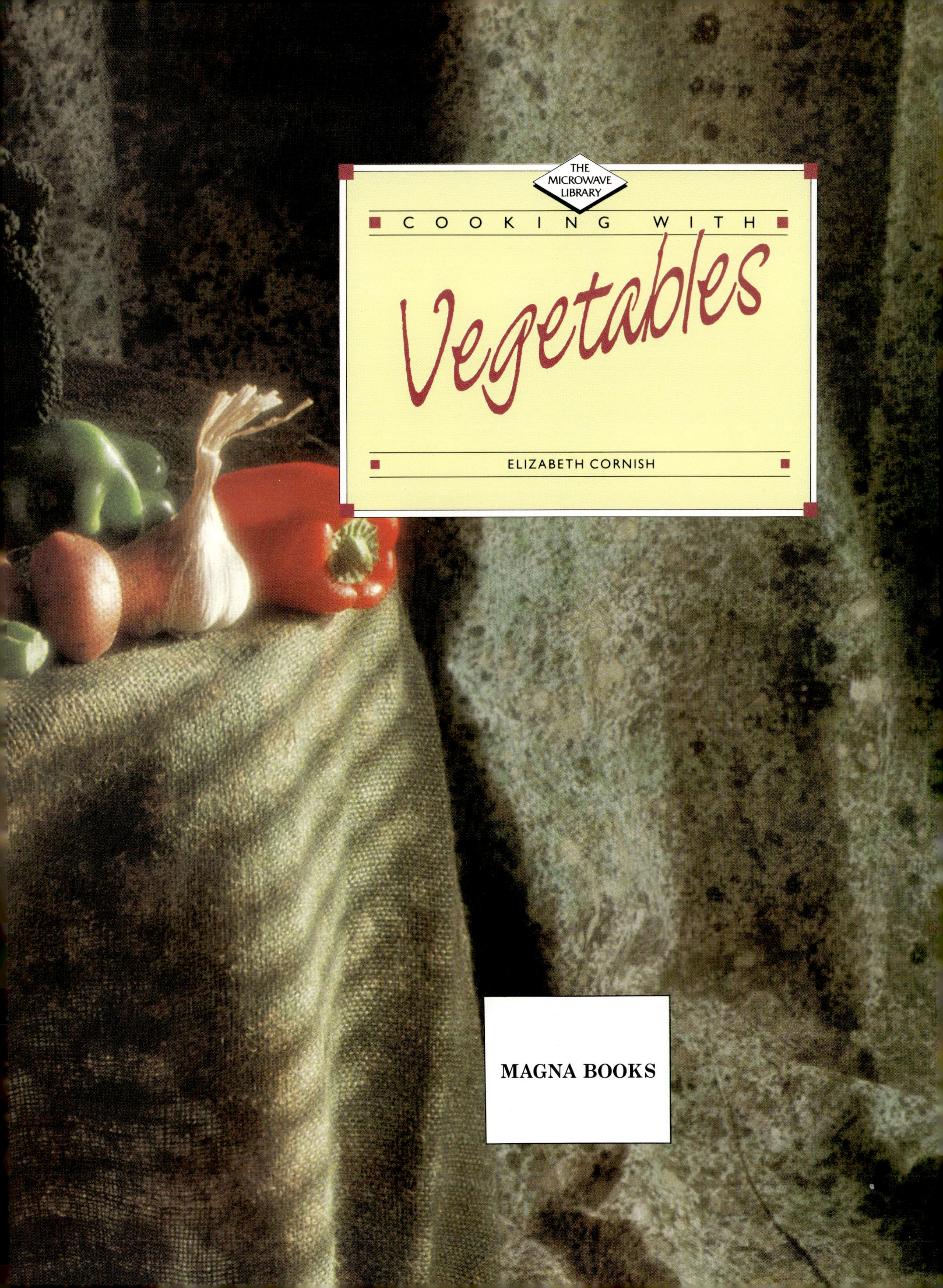

MAGNA BOOKS

A QUINTET BOOK

Published in 1988 by
Magna Books
Magna Road
Wigston,
Leicester, LE8 2XH

ISBN 0 948509 86 4

This book was designed and produced by
Quintet Publishing Limited
6 Blundell Street
London N7 9BH

Art Director: Peter Bridgewater
Photographers: Michael Bull and Trevor Wood
Home Economist: Veronica Bull
Typeset in Great Britain by
Central Southern Typesetters, Eastbourne
Manufactured in Hong Kong by Regent
Publishing Services Limited
Printed in Hong Kong by Leefung-Asco Printers
Limited

CONTENTS

VEGETABLES

VEGETABLES prepared in the microwave are cooked to perfection. They are both tender and crisp and full of flavour and freshness. The vegetables look as if they have been harvested only moments before, because they keep their shape and their colour. They keep their goodness too – research has shown that microwave cooking destroys fewer nutrients than any other method.

These advantages are due to the speed of the microwave, and to the fact that the moisture content of vegetables is high, so that they can be literally cooked in their own juices.

Gone are the days of soggy sprouts and cabbage, when these once perky leaves were boiled until they had collapsed, lost all their colour and flavour and become virtually worthless as a source of nutrient. Now you can cook these and other vegetables in just a few minutes without getting a kitchen full of steam and unpleasant smells that cling to the curtains for days. What you will get is a vegetable looking and tasting like nature intended it to – delicious.

Microwaved vegetables are good for slimmers as well as the generally health-conscious, because they are still high in fibre and even if you are cooking in fat, you need so little of it. For the most part, fat can be avoided.

Bearing in mind that the taste and appearance of the vegetable will not be altered by microwave cooking, you should select only the best specimens. Buy fresh vegetables in season, or frozen vegetables, which are picked and then frozen at their best.

This book will give you plenty of ideas for all kinds of vegetable dishes. Many are meals in themselves; others can be served as light suppers, starters, or as part of a vegetarian meal or an accompaniment to meat and fish.

11:15

A selection of cookware, some of it specially designed for the microwave oven, which is suitable for microwaving.

1 Thorpak cake dish **2** Thorpak casserole dish **3** Microware freezer dishes **4** Roasting dish **5** Thorpak jug **6** Browning dish **7** Minidishes (ramekins) **8** Double microwave serving dish **9** Glass loaf pan **10** Glass casserole with lid **11** Cake or soufflé dish **12** Three-section vegetable dish **13** Browning dish **14** Glass ovenproof dish

ABOUT THE MICROWAVE OVEN

IF YOU are new to cooking with the microwave, the first thing to do is to read the instruction booklet supplied with your model. This will tell you all you need to know about how your cooker works and how to operate it.

Microwave cookers work by emitting concentrated infra red radiation that penetrates and therefore heats food much faster than conventional cookers. They consequently save considerably on cooking time.

The microwave is like any other kitchen appliance that makes life easier for the cook. Once you are used to it, which takes remarkably little time for such a sophisticated gadget, experience will tell you how long it will take to cook or reheat a given dish. If in doubt, always undercook – you can easily add on another minute or so.

To familiarize yourself with the cooker try baking a potato. Scrub the potato and prick the skin a few times with a fork. Lay it on a piece of absorbent kitchen paper and cook on full power for about 6 minutes for a 175 g/6 oz potato. Stop cooking half-way through to turn the potato over. A successfully baked potato will demonstrate how easy microwave cooking is.

Remember to stir or rearrange items during cooking or the food may not be evenly cooked, and

always cover a dish with a lid or cling film (plastic wrap) which you have pierced in two or three places with a knife to make vents through which the steam can escape.

Don't use anything metallic in the microwave, and this includes china decorated with silver or gold leaf. If you want to test if a dish is microwave-proof, put it in the oven next to a cup of water and cook on full for a minute. If the water is hot and the dish stays cool, it is safe to use. If the dish is hotter than the water, avoid using it.

Always prick the skins of vegetables and fish to prevent them from bursting. Eggs should always be pricked for the same reason. Never put an egg in its shell in the microwave – it will explode.

All the recipes in this book are timed for a 700-watt oven, and where the recipe times are not specific, this is to avoid errors. A microwave may be a scientific instrument, but even identical ovens may cook at slightly different rates, and neither cooks nor food can be standardized – no two carrots are the same shape and no two cooks cut them in the same way.

However, the following can be taken as a general guide for ovens with a different power rating from that of the model used in the book. For every minute of cooking time specified in these recipes, add 5 seconds for a 650-watt oven, 10 seconds for a 600-watt oven and 30 seconds for a 500-watt oven. But remember, it is *always* safer to undercook and test.

Crockery, cutlery (flatware, glassware and cookware such as this must NOT be used in a microwave oven.

1 Ceramics with metal decoration **2** Dishes with metal decoration and glazes containing metal **3** Cutlery (silverware or flatware) **4** Metal flan tin and disposable foil bakeware **5** Glassware with metal rim or bands **6** Metal pots and pans **7** Metal bakeware **8** Metal skewers or fondue forks

PUREE OF ROOT VEGETABLES

SERVES 4 / SET: FULL

Ingredients
3 cups/350 g/12 oz carrots, sliced
2¼ cups/350 g/12 oz swede (rutabaga), sliced
45 ml/3 tbsp water
butter to taste
salt and freshly ground black pepper
⅔ cup/150 ml/5 fl oz single (light) cream
snipped chives

◆ Peel the vegetables and slice them thinly. Reserve some of the carrot slices and cut them into star shapes for the garnish.

◆ Put the vegetables in a dish with the water. Cover with vented cling wrap (plastic wrap) and cook for 6–8 minutes, until soft.

◆ Drain the vegetables and purée in the blender with butter to taste. Season the purée and reheat for 1 minute.

◆ To serve, spoon a thin pool of cream onto each of 4 heated plates. Make a small mound of purée on each plate and garnish the surrounding cream with shooting stars made of carrot and snipped chives.

VARIATION You can make this purée with any of the winter root vegetables, such as turnip, parsnip and sweet potato.

ARTICHOKE HEARTS, KIDNEY BEANS AND MUSHROOMS WITH VEGETABLE PUREE

SERVES 4 / SET: FULL

Ingredients
1 onion, sliced
1 clove garlic, crushed (minced)
15 ml/1 tbsp sunflower oil
4 cups/250 g/8 oz mushrooms, wiped and sliced
2 cups/400 g/14 oz tinned (canned) kidney beans
generous cup/200 g/7 oz tinned (canned) artichoke hearts, drained
salt and freshly ground black pepper
fresh coriander (cilantro) or parsley leaves
3/4 cup/175 g/6 oz root vegetable purée (see page 11)

This delicious and rather unusual mixture of flavours is enhanced even further by the tang of fresh coriander (cilantro) leaves when the plant is in season.

◆ Put the onion and garlic in a casserole with the oil, cover and cook for 3 minutes. Stir in the mushrooms, kidney beans – with a little of the liquid from the tin (can) – and artichoke hearts and cook, covered for about 5 minutes, stirring once, until the mushrooms are done and the beans cooked through.

◆ Season to taste with salt and pepper and sprinkle with coriander (cilantro) or parsley leaves.

◆ Serve with vegetable purée.

HOT POTATO SALAD

SERVES 4 / SET: FULL

Ingredients
750 g/1½ lb new potatoes, washed but not peeled
60 ml/4 tbsp water
30 ml/2 tbsp virgin olive oil
15 ml/1 tbsp lemon juice or white wine vinegar
salt and freshly ground black pepper
5 ml/1 tsp dry mustard
1 bunch spring onions (scallions)
1 bunch radishes
about 12 black olives, stoned (pitted)
1 cup/200 g/7 oz tinned (canned) green beans, drained (use cooked fresh beans if in season
chopped chives (optional)

Mix the salad with mayonnaise dressing if you prefer. For less cholesterol, use half and half mayonnaise and yogurt.

◆ Put the potatoes in a dish with the water, cover and cook for about 8 minutes, shaking twice, until done. Do not overcook the potatoes, or they will be spongy.
◆ Drain the potatoes, slice them and return to the dish.
◆ Make a dressing by combining the olive oil, vinegar or lemon juice, salt, pepper and mustard in a screw-topped jar and shaking well. Pour this over the hot potatoes and keep covered.
◆ Trim the spring onions (scallions) and slice down the stalk, making 2 cuts at right angles to each other. Put the onions in iced water for a couple of minutes. The stalks will curl up to make tassels.
◆ Trim and slice the radishes.
◆ Mix the spring onion tassels, radishes, olives, green beans and chives, if liked, into the salad and serve at once.

Hot potato salad

GREEN BEAN AND MUSHROOM CURRY

SERVES 2–4 / SET: FULL

Ingredients
4 tbsp/50 g/2 oz butter or ghee
1 large onion, chopped
2 cloves garlic, chopped
1 cup/100 g/4 oz green beans, trimmed and cut into 2-cm/1-in lengths
2 cups/100 g/4 oz mushrooms, sliced
3 tomatoes, peeled and chopped
1 lb lemon juice
2 slices fresh ginger
2½ ml/½ tsp turmeric
2½ ml/½ tsp ground coriander
2½ ml/½ tsp garam masala
fresh coriander (cilantro) or parsley

◆ Place the butter or ghee in a bowl and cook for 1 minute. Add the onion and garlic and cook for 3 minutes.
◆ Stir in the rest of the ingredients except the fresh coriander (cilantro) or parsley. Cover and cook for 8–10 minutes, stirring twice.
◆ Garnish with fresh coriander or parsley and serve with rice.

STUFFED PEPPERS WITH TOMATO SAUCE

SERVES 4
SET: FULL AND MEDIUM

Ingredients
4 baby peppers, red, green or yellow
60 ml/4 tbsp water
Tomato Sauce
15 ml/1 tbsp oil
1 large onion, chopped
1 clove garlic, chopped
1 carrot, chopped
1 stick (stack) celery, chopped
400 g/14 oz tin (can) tomatoes, with juice
15 ml/1 tbsp tomato purée (paste)
a few sprigs of basil
salt and freshly ground black pepper
Stuffing
1 cup/175 g/6 oz cooked rice
⅓ cup/50 g/2 oz cooked bacon, chopped
⅓ cup/50 g/2 oz salami, chopped
30 ml/2 tbsp chopped parsley
15 ml/1 tbsp tomato purée (paste), diluted with 15 ml/1 tbsp water
salt and freshly ground black pepper

Use baby peppers for this dish. They look much more tempting – and less daunting – than the large ones.

◆ Cut the tops off the peppers and reserve. Scoop out the pith and seeds. Put the peppers and their lids in a deep dish with the water, cover and cook on full for about 7 minutes, rearranging twice. Drain and keep warm.

◆ To make the sauce put the oil in a pot and cook for 30 seconds. Add the onion, garlic, carrot, and celery and cook on full, covered with vented cling wrap (plastic wrap) for 4 minutes.

◆ Stir in the tomatoes, tomato purée (paste) and basil. Cover and cook on full power for 8 minutes, stirring twice. Put the sauce in the liquidizer and blend until smooth. Season to taste.

◆ For the stuffing, mix together the rice, bacon, salami and parsley. Stir in the tomato purée (paste), diluted with water, and season to taste with salt and pepper.

◆ Stuff the peppers with this mixture and put on their lids. Stand the peppers upright in a deep dish, cover with vented cling wrap (plastic wrap) or a lid and cook on medium power for 8–10 minutes, turning the dish 3 times, until the peppers are cooked through and the filling hot.

◆ Remove the lids and serve each pepper in a pool of the reheated sauce.

Parsnips and Mushrooms in a Cheese Sauce

SERVES 4 / SET: FULL

Ingredients
500 g/1 lb parsnips
45 ml/3 tbsp water
15 ml/1 tbsp lemon juice
4 cups/250 g/8 oz mushrooms, wiped and sliced
SAUCE
3 tbsp/40 g/1½ oz butter
6 tbsp/40 g/1½ oz flour
1¼ cups/300 ml/½ pt milk
½ cup/50 g/2 oz grated cheese
salt and freshly ground black pepper
nutmeg

◆ Peel the parsnips, trim them and cut into eighths. Cut away any very woody cores. Put them in a dish with the water and lemon juice. Cover with vented cling wrap (plastic film) and cook for 7 minutes, stirring twice.

◆ Stir in the mushrooms. Cover again and cook for a further 3–4 minutes, until the vegetables are done. Keep hot.

◆ Make the sauce. Put the butter in a dish and cook for 30 seconds. Stir in the flour. Pour on the milk and cook for 3 minutes, whisking after each minute. Stir in the cheese. Cook for a further minute, then whisk again. Season to taste with salt, pepper and nutmeg.

◆ Drain the vegetables and pour the sauce over them. Reheat for a minute if necessary.

NEW POTATOES WITH PEAS AND BACON

SERVES 4 / SET: FULL

Ingredients
500 g/1 lb new potatoes, washed and scrubbed
1 kg/2 lb fresh peas (about 4 cups/500 g/ 1 lb peas shelled weight)
60 ml/4 tbsp water
2 rashers (strips) bacon
⅔ cup/150 ml/¼ pt cream
paprika
mint leaves or chopped chives (optional)

◆ Put the potatoes and peas in a dish with the water, cover and cook for about 8 minutes, shaking the dish twice. Test the potatoes before the cooking time is up. You should not overcook them, or they will go spongy.

◆ Put the bacon rashers (strips) on a grilling (browning) dish, cover with a sheet of kitchen paper to stop them splattering and cook for 1½ minutes. Chop up the bacon and mix it with the vegetables.

◆ Heat the cream in a jug for 1–2 minutes, pour over the vegetables and sprinkle with paprika.

◆ Serve garnished with mint leaves, or chopped chives if available.

Black-eyed Beans (Peas) with Mushrooms and Coriander (Cilantro)

SERVES 4 / SET: FULL

Ingredients
- *2 tbsp/25 g/1 oz butter*
- *1 large onion, chopped*
- *2 cloves garlic, chopped*
- *2¼ cups/500 g/1 lb cooked black-eyed beans (peas)*
- *1½ cups/400 g/14 oz tinned (canned) tomatoes, drained and mashed*
- *1 slice fresh ginger*
- *salt and freshly ground black pepper*
- *garam masala*
- *fresh coriander (cilantro)*

◆ Put the butter in a dish and cook for 45 seconds. Add the onion and garlic and cook, covered, for 3 minutes.

◆ Add the black-eyed beans (peas), tomatoes and ginger and cook, covered, for 4–5 minutes until hot through, stirring once.

◆ Season to taste with salt, pepper and garam masala and stir in plenty of chopped coriander (cilantro) leaves. Eat hot with rice.

◆ This dish is also delicious cold.

Brussels Sprouts with Water Chestnuts, Garlic and Mushrooms

SERVES 4 / SET: FULL

Ingredients
- *1 tbsp/15 g/½ oz butter or margarine*
- *1 clove garlic, crushed (minced)*
- *5–6 cups (approx.)/400 g/14 oz baby Brussels sprouts, trimmed*
- *2 cups/100 g/4 oz mushrooms, sliced*
- *200 g/7 oz tinned (canned) water chestnuts, drained*
- *soy sauce*

◆ Put the butter in a dish and cook for 30 seconds. Add the garlic and cook for 1 minute.

◆ Add the sprouts, mushrooms and water chestnuts, with 15 ml/1 tbsp of the chestnut liquid. Cover and cook for 3–4 minutes, until hot through.

◆ Season with soy sauce and serve.

VARIATION This recipe can also be cooked as for Mixed Vegetable Sauté (see page 23).

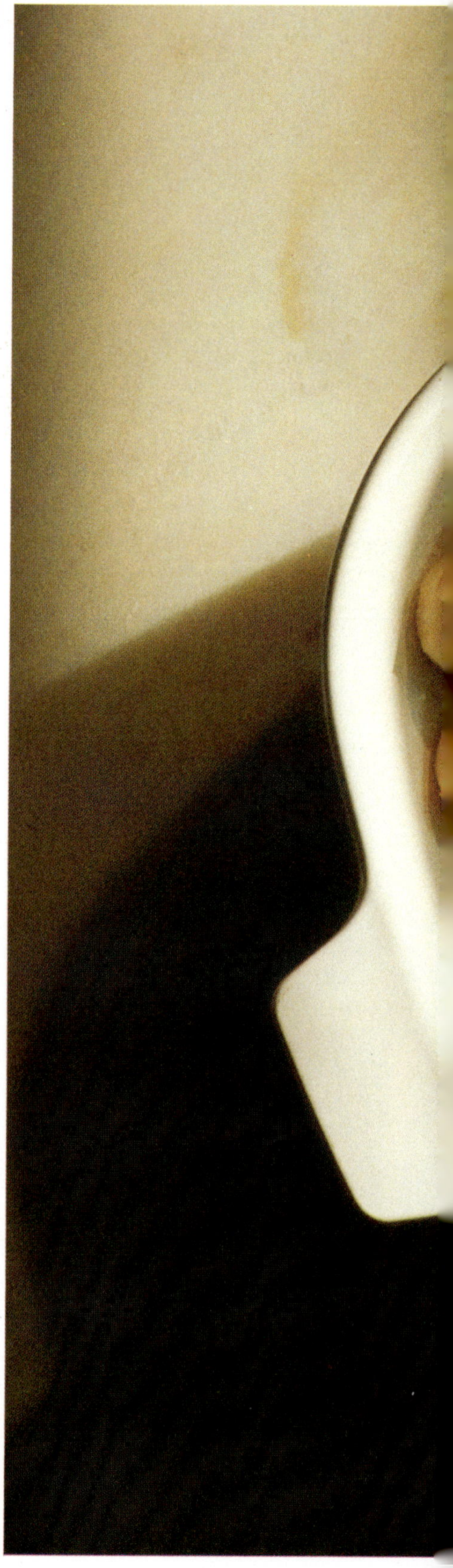

Brussels sprouts with water chestnuts, garlic and mushrooms

LASAGNE WITH RATATOUILLE

SERVES 4 / SET: FULL

Ingredients
Ratatouille
6 sheets spinach lasagne
boiling water
salt
oil
1¼ cups/250 g/8 oz fromage frais (or ricotta)
60 ml/4 tbsp Parmesan cheese

◆ Make the ratatouille according to the instructions on page 61 and keep warm.

◆ Put the lasagne in a deep dish and cover with boiling water. Add a pinch of salt and a few drops of oil, cover with vented cling wrap (plastic wrap) and cook for 15 minutes. Leave to stand for 3 minutes, then drain and rinse thoroughly under cold running water. Lay the lasagne on a tea towel to dry. Do not use kitchen paper – it will stick.

◆ To assemble, put a layer of lasagne in the bottom of an oblong dish, cover with pasta, then spread with fromage frais (or ricotta) and sprinkle with Parmesan cheese. Continue until all the ingredients are used up, finishing with a sprinkling of Parmesan cheese.

◆ Heat through in the microwave or, if you want the top to brown, under the grill (broiler) or in a conventional oven.

MIXED VEGETABLE SAUTE

SERVES 4 / SET: FULL

Ingredients
2 tbsp/25 g/1 oz butter or margarine
1 yellow pepper, seeded and chopped
1¾ cups/100 g/4 oz broccoli florets
½ cup/75 g/3 oz mangetout (snow) peas
1½ cups/75 g/3 oz mushrooms, sliced
50 g/2 oz spring onions (scallions)
soy sauce (optional)

The good thing about using the microwave to cook vegetables together is that they retain their individual flavours.

◆ Heat a browning dish to maximum, according to manufacturer's instructions. Add the butter or margarine and, using oven gloves, tilt the dish so that it is coated with the hot fat.

◆ Put the vegetables in the dish and cook for 2 minutes, stirring once.

◆ Serve with soy sauce and rice.

Mixed vegetable sauté

CHICORY (BELGIAN ENDIVE) IN HAM AND CHEESE SAUCE

SERVES 4 / SET: FULL

Ingredients
4 heads chicory (Belgian endive)
45 ml/3 tbsp water
3 tbsp/40 g/1½ oz butter
6 tbsp/40 g/1½ oz flour
1¼ cups/300 ml/½ pt milk
⅓ cup/50 g/2 oz Parmesan cheese
⅓ cup/50 g/2 oz cooked ham, chopped
salt and freshly ground black pepper

◆ Trim the chicory (Belgian endive) and cut in half lengthways. Lay in a dish and add the water. Cover with vented cling wrap (plastic wrap) and cook for 4–6 minutes, until tender, turning the dish twice.

◆ Make the sauce. Put the butter in a dish and cook for 1 minute. Stir in the flour. Pour on the milk and cook for 3 minutes, whisking after each minute. Stir in the cheese, cook for a further minute and whisk again. Stir in the ham and season to taste.

◆ Drain the chicory, pour over the sauce and heat through for 1 minute.

AUBERGINE (EGGPLANT) LASAGNE

SERVES 4 / SET: FULL

Ingredients
2 medium aubergines (eggplant)
30–45 ml/2–3 tbsp water
6 sheets spinach lasagne
salt
il
to Sauce (see page 16)
SAUCE
½ oz butter or margarine
z plain (all-purpose)
milk
ese, grated
sal… epper

from Mary Larry Ben & Sam.

◆ Slice the aubergines (eggplant). Arrange them in a deep oblong dish, in which you will cook the finished lasagne. Add the water, cover with vented cling wrap (plastic wrap) and cook for 7 minutes, rearranging once, until tender. Drain and set aside.

◆ Put the lasagne in a large deep pot and pour over enough boiling water to cover. Add salt and a few drops of oil to stop the pieces sticking together. Cover and cook for 12–15 minutes, until done.

◆ Tip the lasagne into a colander and rinse thoroughly under running cold water. If you omit this step you are liable to be left with a soggy mass of unmanageable pasta. Lay the sheets to dry on a tea towel. (Don't use paper towels – they will stick.)

◆ To make the cheese sauce put the butter or margarine in a bowl and cook for 1 minute. Stir in the flour. Pour on the milk. Cook for 3 minutes, whisking after each minute. Stir in the cheese. Cook for a further minute and whisk again. Season to taste with salt … pepper.

… assemble the dish start with a … ubergines, then cover with … e, a layer of pasta and a … e sauce. Continue until … edients are used up, … g with a layer of cheese sauce.

◆ … eat through in the microwave, or in a conventional oven or under the grill (broiler) if you want the top to brown.

◆ Serve hot.

VARIATION Omit the pasta for an Aubergine (Eggplant) Layer Bake.

LEEK PARCELS

SERVES 4 / SET: FULL

Ingredients
3 tbsp/40 g/1½ oz polyunsaturated vegetable margarine or butter
6 tbsp/40 g/1½ oz plain (all-purpose) flour
1¼ cups/300 ml/½ pt milk
½ cup/50 g/2 oz grated Edam cheese
5–10 ml/1–2 tsp mustard (optional)
salt and pepper
4 leeks
30 ml/2 tbsp water
4 slices ham

◆ First make the sauce. Put the margarine or butter in a bowl and cook for 1 minute. Stir in the flour. Pour on the milk. Cook for 3 minutes, whisking after each minute. Stir in the cheese and mustard, if used. Cook for a further minute and whisk again. Season to taste with salt and pepper. Keep the sauce warm while you cook the leeks.

◆ Trim the leeks and wash thoroughly. Put them in a dish with the water, cover with vented cling wrap (plastic wrap) and cook for about 8 minutes, rearranging once, until done.

◆ Drain the leeks and cut off a few rings for the garnish. Wrap each in a slice of ham, lay side by side in the dish and pour the sauce over. Cover and cook for 2–3 minutes until hot through.

◆ Garnish with leek rings and serve at once.

FRENCH BEAN SALAD

SERVES 4 / SET: FULL

Ingredients
4 cups approx./500 g/1 lb French beans, trimmed and left whole
60 ml/4 tbsp water
3–4 cups/500 g/1 lb tomatoes, peeled, seeded and cut into strips
22½ ml/1½ tbsp olive oil
22½ ml/1½ tbsp lemon juice
salt and freshly ground black pepper
2 hardboiled (hard-cooked) eggs
chives (optional)

◆ Put the beans in a dish, add the water, cover with vented cling wrap (plastic wrap) and cook for 6 minutes, rearranging twice. The beans should be done but still crisp. Set aside, covered, while you make the dressing.

◆ Mix the oil, lemon juice and seasoning. (Shake them together in a screw-topped jar if you have one handy.)

◆ Drain the beans, mix them with the tomatoes and toss in the dressing.

◆ Separate the whites from the yolks of the eggs. Chop both. Garnish the salad with the egg.

VARIATION If you are feeling artistic, tie the beans into bundles with the chives instead of mixing them together with the tomatoes.

BROCCOLI WITH ALMONDS AND BLUE CHEESE SAUCE

SERVES 4 / SET: FULL

Ingredients
500 g/1 lb broccoli
45 ml/3 tbsp water
2/3 cup/150 ml/1/4 pt cream
6 tbsp/40 g/1 1/2 oz Danish blue cheese
salt and white pepper
scant 1/3 cup/40 g/1 1/2 oz slivered toasted almonds
diamonds of red pepper

◆ Wash the broccoli and remove the outer leaves and tough stalks. Make slits up the stalks to speed up cooking.

◆ Put the broccoli in a dish with the water. Cover with vented cling wrap (plastic wrap) and cook for 10 minutes, rearranging once, until tender. Drain and keep hot.

◆ Mash the cream into the cheese until smooth. Cook for 1–2 minutes. Season with salt and pepper and pour over the broccoli.

◆ Serve garnished with slivered almonds, or with the broccoli florets in a pool of sauce, as shown and decorate with diamonds of red pepper.

Broccoli with almonds and blue cheese

ARTICHOKE HEARTS WITH SPINACH

SERVES 4 / SET: FULL

Ingredients
4 cups/1 kg/2 lb fresh spinach
2 tbsp/25 g/1 oz butter
1 large onion, chopped
8 artichoke hearts, fresh or canned
½ cup/75 g/3 oz Parma ham, cut into strips
SAUCE
3 tbsp/40 g/1½ oz butter
6 tbsp/40 g/1½ oz flour
1¼ cups/300 ml/½ pt milk
⅓ cup/50 g/2 oz grated Parmesan cheese
nutmeg
salt and freshly ground black pepper

◆ Wash the spinach and discard tough stalks and discoloured leaves. Put it in a boiling or roasting bag and tie loosely. Cook for about 6 minutes, shaking the bag once, until the spinach has collapsed. Let it stand for a while, then chop coarsely.

◆ Put the butter in a dish and cook for 30 seconds. Add the onion and the artichoke hearts and cook for 3 minutes. (If using canned artichoke hearts, however, arrange them on top of the onion when cooked.)

◆ Lay strips of Parma ham in between the artichokes and put the chopped spinach in a layer on top of that.

◆ To make the sauce put the butter in a bowl and cook for 30 seconds to 1 minute to melt it. Stir in the flour. Pour on the milk and cook for 3 minutes, whisking after each minute. Add the cheese. Cook for a further minute and whisk again. Season to taste with nutmeg, salt and pepper.

◆ Pour the sauce over the vegetables and heat through in the microwave, or brown in a conventional oven or under the grill (broiler).

AUBERGINE (EGGPLANT) WITH TWO SAUCES

SERVES 4 / SET: FULL

Ingredients
2 medium aubergines (eggplant), sliced
60 ml/4 tbsp water
flour
beaten egg
breadcrumbs
a little butter
Tomato Sauce (see page 16)
Cheese Sauce (see page 25)

◆ Put the aubergines (eggplant) in a dish, add the water, cover with vented cling wrap (plastic wrap) and cook for 7 minutes, rearranging once, until tender. Drain the aubergines.

◆ Dust the aubergine slices with flour, then dip in beaten egg and in breadcrumbs. Push the breadcrumbs on well with your fingers.

◆ Heat a browning dish to maximum, according to the manufacturer's instructions. Add a little butter and, holding the dish with oven gloves, tilt it to cover in the hot fat.

◆ Fry the aubergine slices in batches for 30 seconds on each side, until golden. Keep warm.

◆ Serve with tomato sauce and cheese sauce.

VARIATION Omit the cheese sauce.

Aubergine (eggplant) with two sauces

CAULIFLOWER IN ORANGE SAUCE

SERVES 4 / SET: FULL

Ingredients
1 cauliflower
45 ml/3 tbsp water
2 tbsp/25 g/1 oz butter
3 tbsp/25 g/1 oz cornflour (cornstarch)
$1\frac{1}{4}$ cups/300 ml/$\frac{1}{2}$ pt unsweetened orange juice
finely grated rind of $\frac{1}{2}$ orange
orange bows

This makes a welcome change from cauliflower cheese.

◆ Trim the cauliflower and break into florets. Put them in a dish, add the water, cover with vented cling wrap (plastic wrap) and cook for 8–10 minutes, depending on size, until tender but not soft. Drain and keep warm.

◆ Put the butter in a jug and cook for 30 seconds. Stir in the cornflour (cornstarch) and cook for 1 minute. Stir in the orange juice and cook for 3 minutes, whisking after each minute. Stir in the orange rind.

◆ Serve the cauliflower on pools of sauce, garnished with the orange bows.

PEPPERS AND FRIED EGGS

SERVES 4 / SET: FULL

Ingredients
1 red pepper, cut into julienne strips
1 green pepper, cut into julienne strips
1 yellow pepper, cut into julienne strips
2 large tomatoes, peeled, seeded and cut into strips
1 bunch spring onions (scallions), trimmed
45 ml/3 tbsp water
a knob of butter
4 eggs
salt and pepper

◆ Put the vegetables into a dish with the water, cover with vented cling wrap (plastic wrap) and cook for 4–5 minutes, stirring once, until tender but not soft. Keep warm.
◆ Heat a browning dish for 3–4 minutes. Add the butter and, using oven gloves, tilt the dish to coat with the hot fat. Break an egg into each corner of the dish and pierce the yolks with a cocktail stick (toothpick). Cook until nearly set (about 2½ minutes, but this will depend on the size of the eggs). Allow to stand for 30 seconds.
◆ Divide the vegetables between 4 heated plates and lay an egg on each.
◆ Offer salt and pepper at the table.

VARIATION You can add garlic to the ingredients if you like and, for a touch of style, make the spring onions (scallions) into tassels.

Peppers and fried eggs

PERFECT ASPARAGUS

SERVES 4 / SET: FULL

Ingredients
3 cups/350 g/12 oz asparagus spears
45 ml/3 tbsp water
3 tbsp/40 g/1½ oz butter
30 ml/2 tbsp Parmesan cheese

If you have too little asparagus to go round, serve it with fried eggs, or scrambled eggs and triangles of toast.

◆ Trim the woody ends from the asparagus spears so that they are all the same length. Lay them in a dish arranged top to tail and pour on the water. Cover with vented cling wrap (plastic wrap) and cook for 5–7 minutes, depending on the size of the spears.
◆ Drain the asparagus and keep warm.
◆ Put the butter and Parmesan in a jug and cook for 1 minute
◆ Serve the sauce separately.

RED CABBAGE AND APPLE

SERVES 4 / SET: FULL

Ingredients
6 cups/500 g/1 lb red cabbage, finely shredded
1⅓ cups/250 g/8 oz cooking apples, peeled, cored and sliced
60 ml/4 tbsp red wine vinegar
30 ml/2 tbsp brown sugar
a pinch of mixed spice (sweet baking spice)
salt and freshly ground black pepper

Cooked conventionally, red cabbage turns blue. Microwave it if you want it to keep its crunch and stay red. This combination is very good with pork chops and baked potatoes.

◆ Mix all the ingredients together in a large dish.

◆ Cover and cook for 15 minutes, stirring twice, until tender but still crunchy.

ITALIAN STYLE COURGETTES

SERVES 4 / SET: FULL

Ingredients
3½ cups/400 g/14 oz courgettes (zucchini), sliced
1 small onion, chopped
1 clove garlic, crushed (minced)
1½ cups/45 ml/3 tbsp water
400 g/14 oz tinned (canned) tomatoes, drained and sieved or blended
salt and freshly ground black pepper
45 ml/3 tbsp grated Parmesan cheese

◆ Put the courgettes (zucchini) in a dish with the onion and garlic. Add the water. Cover with vented cling wrap (plastic wrap) and cook for about 7 minutes, until nearly done.

◆ Stir in the.sieved tomato and season with salt and pepper. Cover and cook for 2–3 minutes, until hot through.

◆ Sprinkle with grated Parmesan cheese and serve.

VARIATION You can layer the courgettes with sliced mozzarella cheese and tomato sauce instead of serving them with Parmesan.

BAKED POTATOES WITH . . .

SET: FULL

◆ Wash the potatoes, 1 per person, and prick with a fork to stop the skins bursting. Put them in the oven on a sheet of absorbent kitchen paper. Arrange in a circle if you are cooking several.

◆ Cook for 4 minutes (1 potato weighing about 175 g/6 oz); 6–8 minutes (2 potatoes); or 12–14 minutes (4 potatoes). Turn them over half-way through cooking time.

SUGGESTED FILLINGS

Chilli (Chili) Beans (see page 40)
Blue cheese mashed with cream
Cottage cheese and chives
Grated Cheddar and crispy bacon pieces
Butter melted with garlic and herbs

CHILLI (CHILI) BEANS

SERVES 4 / SET: FULL

Ingredients
1 large onion, chopped
1–2 cloves garlic, chopped
15 ml/1 tbsp sunflower oil
1 fresh green chilli (chili), chopped and seeded
chilli (chili) powder to taste
½ red pepper, seeded and chopped
½ green pepper, seeded and chopped
1½ cups/400 g/14 oz tinned (canned) tomatoes, drained and mashed, juice reserved
4 cups/800 g/2 × 14-oz cans kidney beans, drained
salt
red and green pepper cut into julienne strips
sliced green chillies (chilis) (optional)
triangles of toast

Use as much or as little chilli (chili) powder as you like.

◆ Put the onion and garlic in a casserole with the oil, cover and cook for 3 minutes. Stir in the chilli (chili), chilli (chili) powder, chopped red and green peppers and 60 ml/4 tbsp reserved tomato juice. Cover and cook for 5 minutes.

◆ Stir in the tomatoes and kidney beans, cover and cook for 5 minutes, or until the mixture is hot through, stirring once. Season with salt to taste.

◆ Garnish with julienne of red and green pepper and sliced chillies (chilis) if liked (remember to warn your guests!).

◆ Serve with triangles of toast. This is also good with rice or baked potatoes.

GLAZED ONIONS

SERVES 4 / SET: FULL

Ingredients
8 small onions, peeled but left whole
30 ml/2 tbsp honey
2 tbsp/25 g/1 oz butter
30 ml/2 tbsp hot water

- Put the onions in a dish.
- Cream the honey and butter with the water and pour over the onions. Cover with vented cling wrap (plastic wrap) and cook for 8–10 minutes, until the onions are tender, shaking or stirring the dish once.
- Serve hot. This is particularly good with pork chops and mashed potatoes.

CRUDITES WITH HOT ANCHOVY DIP

SET: FULL

Ingredients	
A selection of crisp raw vegetables, cut into manageable pieces, such as: carrots, celery, green, red and yellow peppers, cucumber, cauliflower and broccoli florets, radishes, mushrooms.	
DIP	
1/2 cup/100 g/4 oz butter, diced	
2 cloves garlic, crushed (minced)	
8 anchovy fillets, pounded	
1 1/4 cups/300 ml/1/2 pt double (heavy) cream	

◆ To make the dip, put the butter in a pot and cook for 1 minute until melted. Add the garlic and cook for 30 seconds.

◆ Put the anchovy fillets with the cream in a liquidizer and blend until smooth.

◆ Pour the anchovy cream onto the garlic butter, stir well and cook for 1–2 minutes, until hot.

◆ Put the pot with the anchovy dip on a large platter and arrange the crudités around it.

Crudités with hot anchovy dip

COUSCOUS WITH VEGETABLES

SERVES 4 / SET: FULL

Ingredients
½ cauliflower, cut into florets
250 g/8 oz carrots, diced
1 large parsnip, diced
45 ml/3 tbsp water
2 cups/400 g/14 oz tinned (canned) chick peas (garbanzos), drained
1¾ cups/200 g/7 oz tinned (canned) peas, drained
Tomato Sauce (see page 16) made with chilli (chili) powder to taste instead of basil
2 cups/350 g/12 oz couscous
2 cups/450 ml/¾ pt boiling water
salt
2 tbsp/25 g/1 oz butter

◆ First prepare the vegetable topping. Put the cauliflower, carrots and parsnip into a dish with the water, cover with vented cling wrap (plastic wrap) and cook for 5 minutes, stirring once.

◆ Stir in the chick peas (garbanzos) and peas and cook for a further 4 minutes, stirring once. Drain and keep hot.

◆ For the couscous, put the grain in a deep pot, cover with the boiling water, add a pinch of salt and cook for 4 minutes. Stir in the butter.

◆ Reheat the tomato sauce for 3 minutes in a sauce boat.

◆ Serve the couscous topped with the spicy vegetable mixture and allow guests to serve themselves with the sauce.

POTATO OMELETTE (OMELET)

SERVES 2
SET: FULL AND LOW

Ingredients
1 cup/100 g/4 oz cooked sliced potato
1 little butter
4 eggs
salt and freshly ground black pepper
freshly chopped herbs or chives (optional)

This is a good way of using leftover potatoes. Add other vegetables, if you like.

◆ Put the potato in 1 or 2 layers in a buttered dish. Use a shallow dish or a pie plate. Cover and cook on full for 45 seconds.

◆ Beat together the eggs, seasoning and chives or herbs if used and pour them over the vegetables. Cook on low power for 8 minutes, or until almost set.

◆ Leave to stand for 1–2 minutes before serving, then cut in two.

◆ Left until cold, then cut into wedges, this makes a good picnic dish especially if served with salad.

NOTE Quite often quiches and omelettes (omelets) won't cook in the 'cold spot' in the middle of the microwave. To correct this place under a hot grill (broiler) for 2–3 minutes.

Lasagne and leek rolls

LASAGNE AND LEEK ROLLS

SERVES 4 / SET: FULL

Ingredients
4 young leeks
boiling water
30 ml/2 tbsp water
4 sheets spinach lasagne
salt
oil
boiling water
2/3 cup/100 g/4 oz ricotta cheese

Use only very young leeks to make this elegant-looking starter.

◆ Trim the leeks and blanch the discarded tops by pouring boiling water over them and leave to stand for 2 minutes. Put to one side. Put the leeks in a dish with 30 ml/2 tbsp water, cover with vented cling wrap (plastic wrap) and cook for 4 minutes, until tender. Drain and allow to cool.

◆ Put the pasta in a deep dish with a pinch of salt and a few drops of oil. Cover with boiling water. Cook for 10 minutes. Let the pasta stand for 2 minutes, then drain and rinse thoroughly under cold running water. Lay the pasta on a tea towel to dry. (Do not use kitchen paper – it will stick.)

◆ When the pasta has cooled, spread each sheet with 1½ tbsp/25 g/1 oz ricotta cheese. Lay a leek at the end of each sheet and roll up tightly.

◆ Trim away any excess leek, and cut the rolls into slices.

◆ Trim the blanched leek tops and arrange on individual plates as shown. Place the slices in the middle and serve cold.

ARTICHOKE RISOTTO

SERVES 4 / SET: FULL

Ingredients
3 tbsp/40 g/1½ oz butter
1 onion, chopped
1½ cups/350 g/12 oz long-grain Italian rice
3 cups/750 ml/1¼ pt boiling water
1 chicken stock (bouillon) cube
4 very small artichokes
salt and freshly ground black pepper
30 ml/2 tbsp Parmesan cheese

To make this risotto you will need very young, very tender artichokes. If these are not available, use tinned (canned) artichoke hearts.

◆ Put half the butter in a deep pot and cook for 30 seconds. Add the onion, cover and cook for 1 minute.

◆ Stir in the rice. Pour over the boiling water and crumble on the stock (bouillon) cube. Cover and cook for 8 minutes.

◆ Meanwhile, prepare the artichokes. Trim off the stalks and remove any tough outer leaves. Slice the artichokes vertically. Stir them into the rice and cook for a further 4 minutes. Let the pot stand, covered, for 7 minutes.

◆ Stir in the remaining butter, season with salt and pepper and stir in the Parmesan cheese.

◆ Serve at once.

TURNIP AND POTATO BAKE

SERVES 4 / SET: FULL

Ingredients
2½ cups/450 g/1 lb turnips, peeled and thinly sliced
3 cups/450 g/1 lb potatoes, peeled and thinly sliced
butter
salt and freshly ground black pepper
60 ml/4 tbsp single (light) cream
chopped chives

◆ Layer the turnips and potatoes in a round dish, dotting each layer with butter and seasoning with salt and pepper. Cover with waxed paper and press well down.

◆ Stand the dish on an inverted plate. Cover and cook for 9 minutes, turning once.

◆ Slowly pour over cream so that it seeps between the layers. Brown slightly under the grill (broiler), garnish with chives and serve.

OKRA WITH TOMATOES

SERVES 4 / SET: FULL

Ingredients
approx. 4 cups/500 g/1 lb okra
vinegar
2 tbsp/25 g/1 oz butter
15 ml/1 tbsp olive oil
15 ml/1 tbsp lemon juice
1 onion, chopped
1 clove garlic, chopped
3–4 cups/500 g/1 lb fresh tomatoes, skinned, seeded and cut into strips
salt and freshly ground black pepper
plenty of chopped flat-leaved parsley or fresh coriander (cilantro)
lemon wedges

Tinned (canned) okra are a perfectly acceptable alternative to the fresh variety, should these be unavailable. Serve this dish with rice.

◆ Cut off the okra stalks without damaging the seed cavity inside. Soak them for 30 minutes in cold water acidulated with a little vinegar. This is to combat the stickiness of the vegetable. Rinse in fresh water and pat dry.

◆ Put the butter, olive oil and lemon juice in a dish, add the onion and garlic and cook, covered, for 3 minutes. Add the okra and tomatoes, cover and cook for 4–5 minutes, until tender.

◆ Season to taste with salt and freshly ground black pepper and sprinkle with parsley or coriander.

◆ Serve with lemon wedges.

Okra with tomatoes

ROMAN SPINACH

SERVES 4 / SET: FULL

Ingredients
4 cups/1 kg/2 lb fresh spinach
7½ ml/½ tbsp oil
7½ ml/½ tbsp butter (approx.)
⅓ cup/50 g/2 oz pine nuts
⅓ cup/50 g/2 oz sultanas (white raisins)
2 rashers (strips) bacon, derinded and diced
1 clove garlic, crushed (minced)
salt and freshly ground black pepper

◆ Wash the spinach and discard tough stalks and discoloured leaves. Put it in a roasting or boiling bag and tie loosely. Cook for about 6 minutes, shaking the bag once, until the spinach has collapsed.

◆ Put the oil and butter in a dish (use more if you want a richer taste), and add the pine nuts, sultanas (white raisins), diced bacon and garlic. Cook for 1 minute.

◆ Meanwhile, shred the spinach. Add it to the dish and toss well. Season with salt and pepper to taste.

◆ Cook for a further minute, covered with vented cling wrap (plastic wrap), to heat through.

DAL

SERVES 4 / SET: FULL

Ingredients
1⅓ cups/250 g/8 oz red lentils
2 cups/450 ml/¾ pt boiling water (approx.)
2 slices fresh ginger
a pinch of turmeric
a pinch of salt
15–30 ml/1–2 tbsp sunflower oil
5 ml/1 tsp mustard seeds
1 clove garlic, crushed (minced)
1 green chilli (chili), chopped
a pinch of garam masala
pitta (pita) bread

◆ Put the lentils in a pot and pour on the boiling water. Add the ginger, turmeric and salt, cover and cook for 12–15 minutes, stirring twice, and adding more boiling water if it threatens to dry out. (Cooking time and amount of water needed depend on age of lentils.)

◆ Leave the pot to stand, covered, while you prepare the dressing.

◆ Put the oil in a jug and cook for 1 minute. Add the mustard seeds, garlic and chilli (chili), cover with vented cling wrap (plastic wrap) (the seeds might shoot out, as they start to pop when very hot) and cook for 2 minutes. Stir into the dal. Stir in the garam masala and serve hot with pitta (pita) bread.

◆ If you have any left over, add a little water to thin it down before reheating.

Dal

BEETROOT (BEETS) WITH CREAM AND MUSHROOMS

SERVES 4 / SET: FULL

Ingredients
2 tbsp/25 g/1 oz butter
1 clove garlic, crushed (minced)
4 cups/250 g/8 oz mushrooms, sliced (or whole button mushrooms)
4 cups/500 g/1 lb beetroot (beets), cooked and chopped
2/3 cup/150 ml/1/4 pt cream
30 ml/2 tbsp grated Parmesan cheese
30 ml/2 tbsp breadcrumbs

◆ Put the butter in a dish and cook for 1 minute to melt it. Add the garlic and mushrooms, cover with vented cling wrap (plastic wrap) and cook for 3–4 minutes, stirring once.

◆ Mix in the beetroot (beets).

◆ Stir the cream and cheese together and pour over the vegetables.

◆ Sprinkle on the breadcrumbs and cover and cook for 4–5 minutes, until hot through.

MARINATED MUSHROOMS

SERVES 4 / SET: FULL

Ingredients
5 cups/500 g/1 lb button mushrooms, wiped
60 ml/4 tbsp olive oil
60 ml/4 tbsp lemon juice
15 ml/1 tbsp coriander seeds
salt and freshly ground black pepper
parsley or coriander (cilantro) leaves
chopped chives (optional)
toast

◆ Put the mushrooms in a dish with the oil, lemon juice and coriander seeds. Let them marinate for an hour or two or in the fridge overnight.

◆ Remove the mushrooms from the marinade with a slotted spoon and place in a shallow dish. Brush with the marinade and cook for 3 minutes, stirring every minute.

◆ Season to taste, sprinkle with parsley or coriander (cilantro), and chives, if liked, and serve with triangles of toast.

Marinated mushrooms

RUSSIAN BEETROOT (BEETS)

SERVES 4 / SET: FULL

Ingredients
6 tbsp/75 g/3 oz butter
5 medium uncooked beetroots (beets), diced
2 tbsp red wine vinegar
2½ ml/½ tsp dried dill
2½ ml/½ tsp dried fennel
salt and freshly ground black pepper
3 tbsp/25 g/1 oz cornflour (cornstarch)
30 ml/2 tbsp milk
fresh dill or fennel
soured (sour) cream

◆ Place butter in a bowl and cook for 1 minute. Stir in beetroot (beets), vinegar, herbs and seasoning. Cover and cook for 8 minutes or until beetroots are tender.

◆ Place cornflour (cornstarch) and milk in a small bowl and mix until smooth. Stir mixture into beets and cook, covered, for about 4 minutes until thickened.

◆ Allow to stand, covered, for 2 minutes. Garnish with fresh dill or fennel and serve hot or cold, with soured (sour) cream, to accompany cold meats.

CABBAGE WITH BACON AND POTATOES

SERVES 4 / SET: FULL

Ingredients
1 curly cabbage, shredded
2 rashers (sirips) bacon, chopped
½ cup/75 g/3 oz Continental sausage, diced
2 cups/250 g/8 oz baby onions, peeled but left whole
⅔ cup/150 ml/¼ pt chicken stock
2 cups/500 g/1 lb potatoes, cooked and mashed
2 egg yolks
butter
milk
salt and freshly ground black pepper

◆ Put the cabbage, bacon, sausage and onions in a dish and pour over the stock. Cover with vented cling wrap (plastic wrap) and cook for about 8 minutes, stirring once, until done.

◆ Purée the potatoes with the egg yolks, adding enough butter and milk to make them smooth and creamy. Season to taste with salt and pepper.

◆ Put the potato purée on top of the cabbage, cover and cook for 3 minutes, or until hot through. If preferred, brown in a conventional oven or under the grill (broiler).

Cabbage with bacon and potatoes

RICE WITH PEPPERS AND CHEESE

SERVES 4 / SET: FULL

Ingredients
1½ cups/350 g/12 oz rice
750 ml/1¼ pt boiling water
1 beef stock (beef bouillon) cube
1 small red pepper, seeded and chopped
1 small yellow pepper, deseeded and chopped
1 small green pepper, seeded and chopped
1 cup/100 g/4 oz Edam cheese, grated
salt and freshly ground black pepper
1 bunch parsley, chopped

◆ Put the rice in a deep pot, pour over the boiling water and crumble on the stock (bouillon) cube. Cover and cook for 8 minutes.

◆ Stir in the green, yellow and red peppers. Cover and cook for 4 minutes.

◆ Stir in the cheese. Check the seasoning and add salt and pepper if necessary (depending on the saltiness of the stock cube). Cover and leave to stand for 5 minutes.

◆ If the cheese has not melted by then, heat through again for 2 minutes.

◆ Stir in the parsley and serve.

Rice with peppers and cheese

ARTICHOKES WITH HOLLANDAISE SAUCE

SERVES 2 / SET: FULL AND MEDIUM OR DEFROST

Ingredients
2 artichokes
30 ml/2 tbsp lemon juice
90 ml/6 tbsp water
HOLLANDAISE SAUCE
¼ cup/50 g/2 oz butter, diced
15 ml/1 tbsp lemon juice
2 small egg yolks
salt and white pepper

◆ Soak the artichokes for an hour or so in a bowl of water acidulated with half of the lemon juice to loosen any soil or grit that may be stuck between the leaves. Rinse thoroughly in clean water and set upside down to drain. Trim off the stalk close to the vegetable so that it stands upright. Remove any damaged outer leaves and rub the cut surfaces with lemon juice. Do not bother to cut the points off the leaves – this is unnecessary and ruins the look of the vegetable.

◆ Put the artichokes upright in a dish, add the water and the remaining lemon juice, cover and cook for 7–8 minutes on full. Tug at one of the lower leaves to see if done. If it promises to come away in your fingers, the artichokes are ready. Leave them to stand for 3 minutes while you make the sauce.

◆ Put the butter in a bowl and cook on medium or defrost for 2 minutes until melted. Add the lemon juice and egg yolks and whisk lightly.

◆ Cook on medium or defrost for 1 minute, whisk again and season.

◆ Drain and serve with the sauce.

◆ To eat the artichoke, pull away the leaves and suck off the tender fleshy part, dipped in the sauce. When you come to the "choke", cut it away and discard it. Eat the heart with a knife and fork – and more sauce.

RATATOUILLE ALLA MOZZARELLA

SERVES 4 / SET: FULL

Ingredients
1 large aubergine (eggplant), sliced
3 courgettes (zucchini), sliced
60 ml/4 tbsp olive oil
1 large onion, sliced
2 cloves garlic, chopped
1 small red pepper, seeded and chopped
1 small green pepper, seeded and chopped
2 cups/100 g/4 oz mushrooms, sliced
425-g/15-oz tin (can) tomatoes, mashed
15 ml/1 tbsp tomato purée (paste)
10 ml/2 tsp fresh mixed herbs, chopped
1 bayleaf
salt and freshly ground black pepper
1 cup/100 g/4 oz mozzarella cheese, cubed

◆ Place aubergine (eggplant) and courgettes (zucchini) in a colander, sprinkle with salt and allow to stand for 30 minutes. Rinse in cold water and pat dry. Cut the aubergine into bite-sized pieces.

◆ Pour the oil into a casserole and cook for 1 minute. Add onion and garlic and cook for 1 minute. Stir in peppers, aubergine and courgettes and cook for 5 minutes, stirring once.

◆ Stir in remaining ingredients, cover and cook for 15 minutes, stirring twice. Stir in mozzarella. Cover and cook for 5 minutes until cheese has melted or brown under the grill (broiler) if preferred. Serve with crusty French bread to mop up the juices.

BABY ONIONS ESCOFFIER

SERVES 4 / SET: FULL

Ingredients
4 cups/500 g/1 lb baby onions
15 ml/1 tbsp oil
1 bay leaf
a sprig of thyme
5 ml/1 tsp fennel seeds
½ cup/50 g/2 oz sultanas (white raisins), soaked
45 ml/3 tbsp dry white wine
15 ml/1 tbsp brandy

◆ Peel the onions, but leave them whole. Put them in a dish with the remaining ingredients, cover with vented cling wrap (plastic wrap) and cook for about 10 minutes, shaking the dish twice.

◆ Serve with lamb, beef or game.

FENNEL WITH PARMESAN

SERVES 4 / SET: FULL

Ingredients
2 bulbs fennel
¼ cup/50 g/2 oz butter
15 ml/1 tbsp lemon juice
salt and freshly ground black pepper
30 ml/2 tbsp Parmesan cheese
30 ml/2 tbsp chopped fresh herbs (optional)

◆ Remove the tough outer leaves of the fennel. Trim the bulbs, but reserve the feathery fronds. Slice the bulbs.

◆ Put the butter in a dish and cook for 1 minute. Add the fennel and turn in the butter to coat. Cover with vented cling wrap (plastic wrap) and cook for about 10 minutes, stirring the dish a couple of times, until the fennel is tender.

◆ Sprinkle on the lemon juice, season with salt and pepper and spoon over the Parmesan cheese.

◆ Garnish with the fennel fronds, chopped, or fresh herbs.

Fennel with Parmesan

BROAD (FAVA) BEANS WITH SWEETCORN (CORN) IN A SPICY CREAM SAUCE

SERVES 4 / SET: FULL

Ingredients
2 tbsp/25 g/1 oz butter
2 cups/200 g/14 oz broad (fava) beans, shelled
2 cups/200 g/14 oz sweetcorn (corn) kernels
30 ml/2 tbsp water
2/3 cup/150 ml/1/4 pt cream
a pinch of ginger
a pinch of cayenne pepper

◆ Put the butter in a dish and cook for 1 minute. Add the broad (fava) beans and sweetcorn (corn) with the water, stir, cover with vented cling wrap (plastic wrap) and cook for 3–4 minutes, until nearly done, stirring once.

◆ Mix in the cream, with ginger and cayenne pepper to taste. Cover and cook for 1 minute.

◆ Serve hot.

NOTE If you want to make an attractive starter of this dish, arrange on individual dishes as shown and pour on the butter. Cover with cling wrap (plastic wrap) and cook for 1½ minutes. Serve the sauce separately.

BUTTERED CARROTS WITH ORANGE

SERVES 4 / SET: FULL

Ingredients
3½ cups/400 g/14 oz baby carrots, scrubbed, with a little bit of leaf, if possible
3 tbsp/40 g/1½ oz butter
30 ml/2 tbsp orange juice
salt and white pepper
orange peel, cut into julienne strips and blanched in water for 1 minute
orange slices

Tiny carrots look and taste much nicer than their large relations, but if you can only get the bigger ones, trim them, peel them and cut into slices. If you manage to find small ones, wash them well, but leave on a few fronds, as they look very pretty.

◆ Put the carrots in a dish with the butter and orange juice, cover and cook for about 10 minutes, until tender. Stir or shake a couple of times during cooking.

◆ Season the carrots with salt and white pepper to taste, or leave this up to your guests.

◆ Serve decorated with the orange peel and slices.

CELERY IN STILTON SAUCE

SERVES 4 / SET: FULL

Ingredients
1 head celery, trimmed and cut into pieces about 5 cm/2 in long (reserve the leaves)
60 ml/4 tbsp water
1 cup/100 g/4 oz ripe Stilton
2/3 cup/150 ml/1/4 pt double (heavy) cream
salt and white pepper
hot toast

◆ Put the celery in a dish and add the water. Cover with vented cling wrap (plastic wrap) and cook for about 10 minutes, until tender. Drain and keep hot.

◆ Crumble the Stilton into the cream. Mash with a fork or blend until smooth in a liquidizer. Season with salt and white pepper. Pour over the celery. Reheat for 1–2 minutes, covered.

◆ Garnish with the celery leaves and serve with hot toast.

Celery in Stilton sauce

CURRIED RICE

SERVES 4 / SET: FULL

Ingredients
2 tbsp/25 g/1 oz butter
1 onion, chopped
1 cup/250 g/8 oz long-grain rice
2½ cups/600 ml/1 pt boiling water
a pinch of salt
5 ml/1 tsp turmeric
2 slices pineapple, chopped
⅓ cup/50 g/2 oz sultanas (white raisins)
⅓ cup/50 g/2 oz dry-roasted peanuts
a pinch of garam masala
30 ml/2 tbsp desiccated (shredded) coconut

◆ Put the butter in a pot and cook for 30 seconds. Add the onion, cover and cook for 3 minutes.

◆ Stir in the rice, pour over the boiling water and add the salt and turmeric. Cover and cook for 10 minutes.

◆ Stir in the pineapple, sultanas (white raisins) and peanuts. Sprinkle on the garam masala and stir that in. Leave, covered, for 5 minutes.

◆ Stir in the desiccated (shredded) coconut and serve.

FRESH VEGETABLES/COOKING GUIDE

vegetables	quantity	minutes on full
globe artichokes	4	10 – 20
asparagus spears	1½ cups/225 g/8 oz	6 – 7
aubergines (eggplant), diced	2 cups/450 g/1 lb	5 – 6
beans, broad (fava, lima), French (green) or runner	2½ cups/450 g/1 lb	8 – 10
beetroot (beets), sliced	4 cups/450 g/1 lb	7 – 8
broccoli florets	6 cups/450 g/1 lb	4 – 5
Brussels sprouts	6 cups/450 g/1 lb	8 – 10
cabbage, shredded	6 cups/450 g/1 lb	7 – 10
carrots, sliced	2 cups/225 g/8 oz	7 – 10
cauliflower florets	6 cups/450 g/1 lb	10 – 11
celery	1 head	10 – 13
corn on the cob	1	3 – 5
courgettes (zucchini), sliced	4	7 – 10
Kohlraki	4 cups/450 g/1 lb	7 – 8
leeks, sliced	4 cups/450 g/1 lb	7 – 10
marrow (squash), sliced	4 cups/450 g/1 lb	8 – 10
mushrooms, whole	2½ cups/225 g/8 oz	5 – 6
okra	4 cups/450 g/1 lb	8 – 10
onions, sliced	2 cups/225 g/8 oz	5 – 7
parsnips, sliced	2 cups/225 g/8 oz	8 – 10
peas	4 cups/450 g/1 lb	7
potatoes, new	6 cups/450 g/1 lb	8 – 10
potatoes, jacket (baked)	2 large	8
potatoes, boiled	4 cups/450 g/1 lb	6 – 7
spinach	2 cups/450 g/1 lb	5
greens, chopped	6 cups/450 g/1 lb	7 – 9
swedes (rutabaga), sliced	3 cups/450 g/1 lb	6 – 7
tomatoes, sliced	1½ cups/450 g/1 lb	2 – 3
turnips, sliced	1½ cups/225 g/8 oz	6 – 7

FROZEN VEGETABLES/COOKING GUIDE

vegetables	quantity	minutes on full
asparagus spears	1½ cups/225 g/8 oz	6 – 7
beans, broad (fava), French (green) or runner	1½ cups/225 g/8 oz	7
broccoli spears	4 cups/225 g/8 oz	6 – 8
cabbage, chopped	3 cups/225 g/8 oz	6 – 7
carrots, sliced	2 cups/225 g/8 oz	6 – 7
cauliflower florets	4 cups/225 g/8 oz	4 – 6
sweetcorn (corn)	2 cups/225 g/8 oz	4 – 6
corn on the cob	1	4 –5
courgettes (zucchini), sliced	2 cups/225 g/8 oz	4
peas	2 cups/225 g/8 oz	4
spinach, chopped	3 cups/225 g/8 oz	5
swedes (rutabaga), cubed	2 cups/225 g/8 oz	7
turnips, sliced	1½ cups/225 g/8 oz	8
vegetables, mixed	2 cups/225 g/8 oz	4 – 6

FRESH MEAT COOKING GUIDE

meat	minutes on full per 450 g/1 lb	standing minutes
bacon (ham) roast	12 – 14	10
bacon, rashers (slices) 4	4½	—
beef, boned roasts, rare	5 – 6	15 – 20
beef, boneless roast, medium	7 – 8	15 – 20
beef, boneless roast, well-done	8 – 9	15 – 20
beef, roasts with bone, rare	5 – 6	15 – 20
beef, roasts with bone, medium	6 – 7	15 – 20
beef, roasts with bone, well-done	8 – 9	15 – 20
beef, ground, 4 patties	10	5
chicken, whole roast	8 – 10	10 – 15
chicken, portions	6 – 8	10
lamb, boned roast	7 – 8	20
lamb, boned and rolled roast	9	20
lamb, roast with bone	6 – 7	20
lamb, crown roast	9 – 10	20
lamb chops	2	10
liver, ox (beef)	8	5
liver, lamb, calves'	7	5
pork, boned rolled roast	8 – 10	15
pork, roast with bone	8 – 9	15
poussin (Cornish rock hen), pigeon, pheasant, quail	5 – 7	5
sausages (links), 4	4	—
portions	15	10
turkey, whole roast	11	10 – 15

FROZEN MEAT DEFROSTING GUIDE

meat	minutes on low per 450 g/1 lb	standing minutes
beef, boned roasts	8 – 10	30
beef, roasts on bone	8 – 10	30
beef, minced (ground)	8 – 10	2
beef steak, cubed	6 – 8	5
hamburgers, two	2	2
hamburgers, four	4	2
chicken, whole	6 – 8	30
chicken portions	5	30
duck and duckling	5 – 7	30
kidney	6 – 9	5
lamb, boned roasts	5 – 6	30 – 45
lamb, with bone	8 – 10	30 – 45
lamb chops	8 – 10	15
liver	8 – 10	5
pork, boned roasts	7 – 8	30
pork roast with bone	7 – 8	45
poussin (Cornish rock hen), grouse, pigeon, pheasant	5 – 7	10
sausages (links)	5 – 6	5
turkey, whole	10 – 12	60
veal, boned rolled roast	5 – 6	30
veal, with bone	8 – 10	45
veal chops	8 – 10	30
veal, minced (ground)	8 – 10	5

FISH
Defrost and Cooking Guide

fish	weight	defrost minutes	standing minutes	cooking in minutes on full
bass	225 g/8 oz	5 – 6	15	5 – 6
bonito tuna steaks,	225 g/8 oz	10	15	—
bream, sea-bream	225 g/8 oz	—	15	10 – 12
cod fillets	225 g/8 oz	4 – 5	5	4 – 6
cod steaks	225 g/8 oz	5	5	6
crab claws	100 g/4 oz	5	5	2 – 3
crab, dressed (crab cakes)	100 g/4 oz	2	10	—
haddock fillets	100 g/4 oz	4 – 5	5	5 – 7
haddock steaks	100 g/4 oz	4 – 5	5	4 – 7
halibut steaks	100 g/4 oz	4 – 5	5	4 – 5
hake steaks	100 g/4 oz	4 – 5	5	4 – 6
kipper (kippered herrings)	100 g/4 oz	—	—	1 – 2
kipper (kippered herrings) fillets (boil-in-the-bag)	200 g/7 oz	3	5	3
mackerel	225 g/8 oz	6 – 8	8 – 10	4 – 5
mahi-mahi	225 g/8 oz	6 – 8	—	4 – 6
red and grey mullet	225 g/8 oz	6 – 8	8 – 10	4 – 6
mussels	225 g/8 oz	5	5	—
plaice (flounder) fillets	225 g/8 oz	4 – 5	5	4
prawns (small shrimp), cooked	225 g/8 oz	5	5	—
red salmon steaks	225 g/8 oz	5	5	4 – 5
scrod fillets	225 g/8 oz	4 – 5	30	4 – 5
scampi (king prawns), raw		5	5	4 – 6
scallops	225 g/8 oz	5	5	5 – 7
snapper	225 g/8 oz	6 – 8	8 – 10	5 – 7
sole	225 g/8 oz	5 – 6	8 – 10	4
trout	225 g/8 oz	6 – 8	8 – 10	7
yellowtail	225 g/8 oz	6 – 8	8 – 10	7

TIME AND SETTINGS FOR PASTA AND GRAINS

Although there are no real time savings in cooking rice and pasta in the microwave, it may be a more foolproof way of cooking as there is no risk of sticking to the pan. Standing is usually necessary to complete cooking.

Cooking times will vary according to the type of pasta. Fresh pasta needs microwaving for only 1 minute. It requires no standing time, but should just be drained and served immediately. Times for dried pasta and rice are given below.

PASTA AND GRAINS COOKING GUIDE PER 225 G/8 OZ

food	boiling salted water to add	cooking in minutes on full	standing minutes
long grain rice (1 generous cup)	3 cups/725 ml/1¼ pt	14	5
pudding (Carolina) rice (1 generous cup)	2½ cups/600 ml/1 pt		
American (converted) rice (2½ cups)	2½ cups/600 ml/ 1 pint	12	5
brown rice	3½ cups/900 ml/ 1½ pt	30	5
egg noodles & tagliatelle (fettucini) (6 cups)	4 cups/1 litre/1¾ pt with 2 tsp oil	6 – 8	2 – 3
spaghetti	4 cups/1 litre/1¾ pt with 2 tsp oil	12	5 – 10
pasta shells (2 cups) & shapes	4 cups/1 litre/1¾ pt with 2 tsp oil	12 – 14	5 – 10
macaroni (2 cups)	4 cups/1 litre/1¾ pt with 2 tsp oil	12 – 15	2 – 3
lasagne (6 cups)	4 cups/1 litre/1¾ pt with 2 tsp oil	9	2

CAKES, BREAD AND DESSERTS DEFROSTING GUIDE

product	quantity	minutes on low	standing minutes
bread, whole loaf	1 large	6 – 8	5 – 15
bread, whole loaf	1 small	4 – 6	10
bread, sliced loaf	1 large	6 – 8	10
bread, sliced loaf	1 small	4 – 6	5
bread slice	25 g/1 oz	10 – 15 secs	1 – 2
bread rolls, crumpets,	2	15 – 20 secs	1 – 2
scones (biscuits), etc	4	25 – 35	1 – 2
cakes, cream	2	45 – 60	10
	4	1¼	10
cakes, small	2	30 – 60	5
cupcakes	4	1¼ – 1¾	5
cakes, large:			
sponge (yellow) cake	450 g/1 lb	4	10
cheesecake	23 cm/9 in	3 – 4	20
dough, pizza and bread	450 g/1 lb	4	10
dough, shortcrust and puff	227 g/8 oz	4	20
dough, shortcrust and puff	397 g/14 oz	6	20
mousse (soufflé), small	1	30 secs	15
pie, fruit or cream	650 g/26 oz	5	10
trifle	1	1	15